Dick King-Smith

Hairy Hezekiah

Illustrated by John Eastwood

HAIRY HEZEKIAH
A YOUNG CORGI BOOK 978 0 552 55256 1 (from January 2007)
0 552 55256 9

First published in Great Britain by Doubleday,
an imprint of Random House Children's Books

Doubleday edition published 2005
Young Corgi edition published 2006

1 3 5 7 9 10 8 6 4 2

Palimpsest Book Production Limited, Polmont, Stirlingshire

Young Corgi Books are published by Random House Children's Books,
61–63 Uxbridge Rd, London W5 5SA,
a division of The Random House Group Ltd,
In Australia by Random House Australia (Pty) Ltd
20 Alfred Street, Milsons Point, Sydney, NSW 2061, Australia,
in New Zealand by Random House New Zealand Ltd,
18 Poland Road, Glenfield, Auckland 10, New Zealand
in South Africa by Random House (PTY) Ltd,
Isle of Houghton, Corner of Boundary Road & Carse O'Gowrie,
Houghton 2198, South Africa

THE RANDOM HOUSE GROUP Limited Reg. No. 954009
www.kidsatrandomhouse.co.uk

A CIP catalogue record for this book is available from the British Library.

Printed and bound in Great Britain by
Mackays of Chatham plc, Chatham, Kent

CHAPTER ONE

In a zoo in an English city there lived a camel. Do not think that I am just a liar, when I say his name was Hezekiah. It really was, honestly. He was a Bactrian camel, very big and heavy and covered in a lot of dark brown hair. On his back he carried two large humps. He was well fed and kindly treated, but in one way Hezekiah was different from all the other animals in the zoo.

They had friends to talk to – the lions in the Lion House, the gorillas and chimpanzees in the Ape House, the birds in the Aviary, the monkeys in the Monkey Temple – they all had others of their kind with them or close by. They could roar or scream or whistle or chatter at one another as much as they liked.

But there were no other camels for Hezekiah to make friends with. He was the only one, and he lived in a wire-fenced grass paddock all by himself.

Hezekiah, you will have guessed, was lonely.

Visitors to the zoo came and stood by the fence and looked at Hezekiah. They could hear him making deep grumbly noises as he stared out at them through his heavily lashed eyes, but they could not know that he was in fact talking to himself out loud.

He had fallen into this habit because he had no camel friends to speak to, no camel voices to listen to, and, though he didn't suppose the humans could understand him, it comforted him to speak his thoughts to the watching people.

"Wish I had a pal," he often said. "Don't suppose you care but I'm the only camel in the zoo, did you know that?"

Often, in reply to Hezekiah's growling and snorting and the bubbly sounds that he made

3

through his thick rubbery lips, the visitors made noises too. But of course Hezekiah could not understand what they were saying to him and anyway he couldn't hear much of it because his ears were very hairy inside.

*

One day Hezekiah was standing by the gate into his paddock, staring out through his heavy eyelashes. It was a bitterly cold winter's day. There were hardly any visitors in the zoo and none at all near him.

He didn't mind the cold a bit as his coat was so thick, but he was more than usually grumpy because he hadn't yet been fed.

"Where's my flipping breakfast?" he growled. "I'm starving. My humps feel all floppy."

Camels store fat in their humps, and if they are really really short of food, the humps shrink in size. Hezekiah wasn't actually starving, of course, just hungry.

When at last he saw his keeper approaching, carrying a bale of hay, he shouted rudely at the man. "Get a move on, slowcoach!" he boomed. "You're late and I'm famished!"

The keeper was a fairly new one who hadn't been at the zoo for long. The only thing he knew about the camel was that he seemed to be a bad-tempered old thing who was always moaning and groaning.

"Keep your hair on, Hezekiah," he said as he slid back the metal bar that kept the gate shut. Now he opened it, threw in the haybale and cut its strings. "There you are, old misery-guts," he called, and he went out again, closing the gate behind him.

Hezekiah tucked into his hay greedily, swallowing it down in great lumps. Like a cow, he would later lie down and chew the cud. When night fell,

he got to his feet and, on his huge splayed hooves, lumbered over to the gate of the paddock and stood, as he often did, staring out.

There was no one for him to talk to, for all the visitors had left the zoo, so, as usual, he talked to himself.

"I wish," said Hezekiah, "that I could open this gate. I could have a walk around the place, meet some other animals, make a pal perhaps, even though I'm the only camel in the zoo. I wonder

7

if I could somehow open the blooming thing. Perhaps it's something to do with that metal bar. Maybe I could shift it."

He lowered his long neck and with his thick blubbery lips he mouthed at the bar. It was stiff and for a while he could not move it. "Easy enough for keepers with fingers and thumbs," he grumbled, "but not for Bactrian camels."

He was on the point of giving up, but then he said to himself, "Oh, come on, Hezekiah, one last go." He gave it one last go and at last the bar slid across and the gate swung open. "Bless my humps!" he said, and walked out.

CHAPTER TWO

The whole of the zoo was dark now, except for lights in a few of the buildings. As Hezekiah made his way towards the nearest one, he heard from within it a deep rolling roar that ended in

a couple of grunts. So he made his entrance through the half-open door into the Lion House.

Now, people cannot understand camel talk and camels can't understand human language. But in one way almost all animals are cleverer than humans, because they can understand one another. To Hezekiah the noise that the lion was making meant "I am the lion, the King of Beasts, and I'm shut up in this horrible cage. Damn and blast!"

The camel made his lumbering way into the dimly lit Lion House and walked along in front of the row of cages. At the sight of him, there was a burst of noise from within them.

"Mum! Mum!" cried some cubs. "Whatever is that thing? Will it hurt us?"

"Of course not," replied a lioness. "First, it can't get into our cage, and second, if it could, I'd kill it and we'd eat it."

"And so would we if only we could get out of our cages," growled several lions.

"But what is it, Mum?" said the cubs.

"Ask it," said their mother.

So they did.

Hezekiah stopped and stood, looking into that cage. He didn't like the smell of the lions, so he closed his nostrils as all camels can. He didn't like the sight of them either, with their gleaming teeth and sharp claws, and certainly he didn't like what they had said they wanted to do to him.

But the bars of the cages looked nice and strong, thank goodness, and, in reply to the cubs' question, he said, "Good evening" (for politeness costs nothing). "I am a Bactrian camel."

"Bactrian camel?" said one of the cubs. "What have you got on your back?"

"Two humps."

"What's in them?"

"Fat," said Hezekiah, and all the lions licked their lips.

The biggest of the lions came forward to the front of his cage.

"What are you doing in here?" he asked. "Why aren't you in the Camel House?"

"There isn't one," said Hezekiah. "I live in a paddock."

"Well, why aren't you there?"

"I've escaped," replied Hezekiah, and a huge sigh of envy rippled through the Lion House.

"How did you manage that?" asked the lion, moving closer to the bars. "Oh, and come a little closer, will you? I'm a bit deaf."

I'm not that stupid, thought Hezekiah.

"Tell you some other time," he said, and he turned and hurried out of the Lion House.

He walked along a path to the next building, which was the Ape House, and made his way inside. In the first cage was a big gorilla.

"Good evening," said Hezekiah.

"Is it?" replied the gorilla. "Why?"

"I've escaped."

"All right for some," said the gorilla gloomily.

"Forgive me for asking," said Hezekiah, "but you don't want to eat me, do you?"

13

"Eat you? No, I'm a vegetarian."

"Oh, sorry," said Hezekiah, and he moved on to the next cage, in which were two chimpanzees.

"We heard that," said one.

"And before you ask," said the other, "we are also mostly vegetarians. But now and again we do like a nice bit of monkey-meat."

"But not camel-meat?" wondered Hezekiah.

"What's a camel?" asked the first chimp.

"I am."

"Oh," said the second. "No, thanks." He shouted down to the other chimpanzee cages. "Would any of you chaps like to eat this fellow?" and in reply there were loud screams of laughter.

Hezekiah could still hear the chimpanzees laughing as he made his lumbering way along to the next building in the zoo, which was the Aviary. Inside, almost all the birds were silent, asleep on their perches, though there were some owls who hooted softly at sight of the intruder.

"Who? Who?" they said. "To wit, who?"

"Evening," said the camel. "My name's Hezekiah. I'm a Bactrian camel."

"Hard luck!" said a voice.

Hezekiah peered in and saw a grey parrot staring at him.

"Why do you say that?" he asked.

"Look in the mirror," said the parrot.

I've been threatened, thought Hezekiah, then laughed at, and now insulted. What next?

He made his way out of the Aviary and walked towards the Monkey Temple. This was a big round pit, inside which were flights of circular steps leading up to a stone building in the centre. It had a domed top and looked something like an Eastern temple.

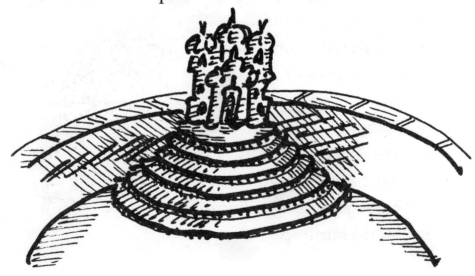

Hezekiah peered over the edge of the wall that surrounded the pit. He could see no monkeys, either on the floor or on the steps. "Good!" he said loudly. "There's no one about to be rude to me."

At the sound of his deep booming voice, a number of little heads popped out of the small windows in the Temple, and he heard a chorus of angry shouts.

"Be quiet!"

"Push off!"

"Sling your hook!"

"Hold your tongue!"

"Shut your trap!"

As he trudged away from the Monkey Temple, Hezekiah began to think that escaping wasn't much fun. "I wanted to make some friends," he said gloomily to the surrounding darkness. "At least nobody was being nasty to me in my own paddock. I wonder what's the next place I shall come to?"

Even as he said this, he saw a single-storey building looming up ahead of him. It seemed to be divided into two halves, each half having a door.

"I wonder who lives here?" he said.

Hezekiah could not read, of course. Had he been able to, he would have seen a notice above each door.

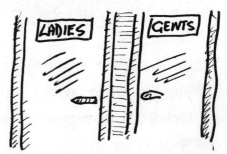

LADIES, one said, and the other GENTS.

CHAPTER THREE

Camels can go a long time without drinking. When they do drink, they can put down an awful lot of water, as much as sixty litres in one go.

As Hezekiah neared the public toilets, his nose told him that there were no animals inside this building, but he could smell water and he realized that he badly needed some.

He'd been so busy earlier grumbling about his food being late that he hadn't had a drink from the trough in his paddock. Now, after what he'd had to put up with in the Lion House and the Ape House and the Aviary and the Monkey Temple, he was very thirsty.

By chance Hezekiah picked the door marked GENTS and somehow squeezed himself through it. To one side was a row of four cubicles, and inside each there stood on the floor a large white basin with a plastic seat on it and a kind of tank above it.

Hezekiah stretched out his long neck to reach one of the basins. It had water in it and he drank greedily till the basin was empty. He did this to each of the four basins in turn till all were empty, but he was still thirsty.

There was a lever sticking out of the tank above each basin, and Hezekiah, out of curiosity, gripped a handle in his mouth and turned it. Immediately

21

there was a rush of water that filled the basin again.

So Hezekiah drained it and turned the handle again and filled the basin and drained it again, on and on, till he was full as much water as he could manage.

Then he squeezed himself out of the GENTS backwards. The wind was cold on that side of the toilet block, so Hezekiah moved round and squeezed himself into the LADIES. He lay down on the floor and went to sleep.

He was woken by a loud scream as an early morning cleaner came in and got the shock of

her life when she bumped
into something large
and hairy.

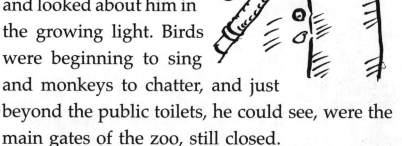

As the cleaner
dropped her mop and
ran away, Hezekiah
got to his feet, gave
himself a good shake
and looked about him in
the growing light. Birds
were beginning to sing
and monkeys to chatter, and just
beyond the public toilets, he could see, were the
main gates of the zoo, still closed.

"I've escaped from my poky little paddock,"
said Hezekiah (not too loudly in case there was
someone about), "but I am still a prisoner. If only
someone would open those gates. Oh, how I wish
they would!"

Maybe there is a special deity that looks after camels, or maybe it was just sheer luck, but at that very moment one of the keepers came out of the lodge beside the gates, and opened them, to be ready in good time for the first of the day's visitors. Even more fortunately, he then went back inside the lodge.

Camels, even great big clumsy Bactrian camels, can move quite fast when they want to. Hezekiah left the shelter of the LADIES and GENTS and was

out through those gates in a flash. His great padded hooves made no sound, and, in a final piece of luck, there was just at that moment no passing traffic on the road outside the zoo. Hezekiah hurried across it into the shelter of some trees.

Looking ahead, he could see green slopes of downland, empty of people at that early hour.

Hezekiah shambled on up them, anxious to get as far as possible from the zoo!

By now the world was waking up, and the

noise of cars and lorries could be heard on the roads below, and then some humans appeared, jogging towards him. Luckily there was a large hollow in the grass nearby, and quickly Hezekiah lay down in it, his neck stretched out flat on the ground, long-lashed eyes and nostrils shut. Had he had 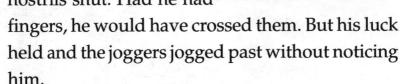 fingers, he would have crossed them. But his luck held and the joggers jogged past without noticing him.

When they had gone, Hezekiah got to his feet and looked about him. Not far away he saw a thick clump of trees.

"Better get in there," he said. "Less chance of

being seen and plenty of leaves to eat. I'll stay there all day and move on when it's dark again. I don't want anyone to see me."

He chomped away at leaves throughout the day until eventually he came to the other side of the clump of trees and found himself on the edge of a garden. In the middle of the garden was a pond where a fountain spurted. Hezekiah wasn't thirsty but he was curious. There didn't seem to be anyone about, so he made his way to the pond.

Inside were a lot of goldfish and they rose to the surface at the sight of the hairy face above them. They opened their mouths in big round "O" shapes and

27

it seemed to the camel that they were all saying, "Who? Who?"

"Actually I'm a Bactrian camel," said Hezekiah. "Don't suppose you've ever seen anything like me before. Can't stop, I'm afraid, in case someone else sees me."

But someone else did see him. It was getting dark by now and in the house at the end of the garden there were two small girls looking out of their bedroom window. They were twins called Josie and Milly, and they very often said the same things at the same time. Now they suddenly saw a large dark shape standing by the goldfish pond.

"Whatever's that?" they said.
"Look at its humps, it's a camel," they said, as Hezekiah moved back towards the shelter of the trees.

"Only one place it could have come from," said Josie.

"And that's the zoo," said Milly.

"It's escaped," they said together.

Then they heard their mother's footsteps coming up the stairs.

"Don't let's tell her," said Josie.

"She wouldn't believe us anyway," said Milly.

Later Hezekiah made his way on across country, avoiding roads and houses, and when dawn broke the following morning, he found

himself in the middle of a large field. A number
of strange shapes surrounded him.

They were animals, he could now see, but
animals such as he had never set eyes on before.
They were quite large, though much smaller
than him, and all were black and white in colour.
They looked curiously at the camel out of their
mild eyes. Hezekiah did not feel threatened by
these strange
beasts.

"Excuse me," he said. "What are you?"

The animals looked at one another, shaking their heads in bemusement.

"Don't you know?" asked one.

"No."

"We'm Friesians."

"What's a Friesian?"

"A cow."

"What's a cow?" asked the camel. "I've never seen animals like you before."

"We ain't never seen no animals like you before neither," mooed all the cows. "What on earth are you?"

"I'm a Bactrian camel," said Hezekiah.

"Come from Bactria, do 'ee?"

"I suppose so. Like you come from Friesia, I imagine."

Before they say something nasty about me, he thought, I'd better say something nice about them.

"You're very pretty," he said. "Can I ask you something?"

"Go on then," said one of the Friesian cows.

"Well, what are those big things between your back legs? Big things with four other things sticking out?"

"Udders," they said. "What be them girt things on your back?"

"Humps," said the camel. "I store fat in them. What's in your udders?"

"Milk," they said.

"What for?"

"For people to drink. They do milk us."

People, thought Hezekiah. I don't want them to see me, they'd put me back in the zoo. He decided he'd ask the cows' advice, politely of course.

"I wonder," he said, "if you can help me. You see, I've just escaped from the zoo and I don't want to go back there. I want to find somewhere safe to go, somewhere with lots of space. Do you know of anywhere?"

The cows looked at one another. Then they looked again at the large dark hairy humped figure of the camel. Then one cow came closer to Hezekiah and said, "You'm in luck, my friend. There's a place not far from yur where they do keep all kinds of curious critturs. That's where you do want to go, I reckon."

"Oh," said Hezekiah. "What is this place?"

The cow replied, "'Tis the safari park."

33

CHAPTER FOUR

"Safari park?" said Hezekiah. "What does that mean?"

"Well," said the cow, "we ain't never bin there, of course, but we do hear tell that 'tis a fine place to live."

"Plenty of room for everyone," said another.

"Bit different from your old zoo, I daresay," said a third.

"How do I get there?"

The whole herd of

Friesians turned to look in one particular direction.

"See them hills in the distance?" they said. "With a good few trees on 'em?"

"Yes," replied Hezekiah.

"That's the edge of the safari park."

"Oh thanks, thanks!" cried Hezekiah. "I'll go on straight away, if you'll all excuse me."

"But you can't get out of this field," they all

said, "till the farmer opens the gate to fetch us in for morning milking."

"Oh I don't need a gate," said the camel. "I'll go out the same way as I came in. Through the hedge."

What a day it was for the farmers of that part of Somerset! Since he had left the Downs in the darkness, Hezekiah had wreaked a trail of havoc through the countryside. Hedges and fences and gates that kept cows and sheep and horses in were no match for the size and strength of the camel. He simply smashed his way through them.

Worse, it was a Sunday, and though farmers work a seven-day week, fifty-two weeks of the year, they do expect to take things a bit easier on a Sunday.

But after Hezekiah burst out again through the

far hedge of the Friesians' field, there was chaos in his wake all through that part of the West Country. Everywhere livestock had taken advantage of the camel's bulldozing passage. Dairy cows, beef cattle, sheep, horses and ponies – all found themselves free to leave their pastures and paddocks and go wherever they pleased.

Farmers can curse as well as most people, but never had there been heard such dreadful cursing as on that Sunday morning. Everyone tried to round up their strays and get them back home and mend the broken gates, the smashed fences, the great camel-sized holes in the hedges.

Hezekiah's Friesian friends were a good example of the fearful confusion for they all went out through the gap that he had made and mingled happily with a neighbouring herd of Ayrshire cows in the next field. It took so long for their angry owners to sort them all out that morning milking did not start till the afternoon.

Hezekiah meanwhile made steady destructive progress towards his goal, crossing, though he did not know it, from Somerset into the county of Wiltshire. He was filled with curiosity about this strange place called a safari park. What would it be like? At last he broke out into a road, a small country lane bordered by trees. Ahead of him was a junction, at which a signpost stood. SHORTSEAT, it said.

Hezekiah hesitated. "Is that the way to the safari park?" he asked himself, and then he heard in the distance the answer to his question. It was a deep rolling roar that ended in a couple of grunts.

39

Chapter Five

The great country house of Shortseat was the ancestral home of a noble family. The present Marquess of Basin had inherited the estate on the death of his father, who had turned his well-wooded lands into a safari park. First he introduced lions. Later he brought in other kinds of interesting and attractive animals that would

normally be found behind bars in zoos. But it was the lions of Shortseat that first attracted the public in great numbers.

As well as coming to see the animals, they came to look round the great house, and on that Sunday afternoon it was filled with people. The present Marquess of Basin moved easily among them, chatting with the visitors, most of whom felt honoured to be addressed by such a great nobleman.

This Lord Basin was (like Hezekiah) an extremely hairy person, and he chose to wear very colourful clothes, as though to mark himself out from the common herd.

On this day he was dressed in sky-blue corduroy trousers,

41

a pink shirt with an emerald-green cravat, and a black velvet jacket lavishly embroidered with gold thread.

At that moment a servant came up to the Marquess. "My Lord," he said, "you are wanted on the telephone."

"Will you forgive me?" said Lord Basin to the visitors (for politeness costs nothing). "I fear I must leave you."

"Of course," murmured some, while many others, unsure of how properly to address the nobleman, replied, "Of course, sir" or "Of course, Your Lordship" or "Of course, Your Grace" and one small boy said, "Yes, Your Majesty."

The Marquess of Basin made his way to his study, where his estate manager was waiting, phone in hand.

"It's the police, sir," he said.

"Whatever do they want?" asked Lord Basin. He took the phone. "Hullo?" he said.

"Lord Basin?" said a voice.

"Speaking."

"Sorry to bother you, my Lord, but we were wondering if any of your animals had escaped? It would be a large one by the look of things."

"Escaped?" said the Marquess. "Animals don't escape from Shortseat, they're too happy here. What animals have you found?"

"None, my Lord," replied the policeman, "but we are getting reports of widespread damage in that part of Somerset to the west of you. Everywhere farmers and landowners are reporting broken gates and fences and big holes through hedges, and they suspect that something large

43

and strong may have escaped from Shortseat. There are fears that it might be one of your lions."

"Rubbish!" said Lord Basin loudly. "Lions don't break gates and make holes in hedges. Sounds more like a camel to me."

"Very good, my Lord," said the policeman, and rang off.

Many years ago, when Lord Basin was a boy, his father had taken him on a visit to the very city zoo from which Hezekiah had escaped, and he had ridden on a Bactrian camel.

He'd never forgotten the sensation of sitting between those two great humps as the camel swayed along the paths of the zoo.

When he was a young man, he heard that

that camel had died of old age. When later he inherited Shortseat, he vowed that he would one day have a camel there. But they were very rare. Only a thousand or so still survived in Mongolia's Gobi desert.

"You haven't had any report of anything escaping, have you, John?" said Lord Basin to his manager.

"No, sir."

"Well, whatever's caused all this damage, it's nothing to do with me."

Even as Lord Basin spoke, Hezekiah was approaching the main gate of the Shortseat Safari Park.

Lord Basin sat back in his office chair, stroking his beard thoughtfully. Maybe the feel of it made him think of hairy creatures.

"Switch on the television, John, please. I want to watch the West Country News."

How I'd love to have a Bactrian camel, he thought, and to his utter amazement the first item on the news was about the escape of a camel from the zoo. It had set off across country, the newscaster said, ending up at Shortseat.

Maybe there is a special deity that looks after marquesses, but at that very moment Hezekiah passed through the gates into Shortseat before the astonished eyes of the gatekeeper and a number of visitors who were about to enter.

With slow steps (for he was now somewhat

hoof-sore) he made his rolling, dignified way, his humps swaying a little, down the long, straight avenue that led to the great house.

Frantically, the gatekeeper telephoned the manager.

Hastily, the manager told the Marquess.

Excitedly, the Marquess made his way through the visitors to the front doors of Shortseat and stood, in his colourful raiment, at the top of the stone steps that led up to the entrance. Behind him, faces peered from every window, witnesses to the arrival of Hezekiah at Shortseat.

They saw the great hairy Lord standing at the top of the steps. They saw the great hairy camel at the bottom.

Hezekiah was very tired now, for he had travelled a long, long way, and he had no intention of trying to climb those steps. Like all camels, he had horny kneepads to rest upon.

So, to the delight of all and in particular of the owner of Shortseat, Hezekiah the Bactrian camel knelt before the Marquess of Basin.

CHAPTER SIX

Later the curator of the zoo rang up. He and the Marquess were old friends, but still there was an edge to his voice as he said, "You've nicked my Bactrian camel!"

"I haven't nicked him," said Lord Basin. "He wasn't invited here, he's just a gatecrasher."

"You can say that again," remarked the

curator. "It's going to cost us thousands of pounds to repair the damage."

The Marquess pulled at his beard thoughtfully.

"Look," he said. "I'll pay for the damage."

"Really? That's very good of you."

"On one condition."

"What's that?"

"You let me keep him."

There was a pause, and then the curator said, "It's an idea. But I think we'd need a bit of icing on the cake. What can you offer in return for him?"

"A zebra?"

"Oh no."

"A giraffe?"

"No."

"How about a white tiger?" said Lord Basin.

"It's a deal!"

"Good. By the way, what's the camel's name?"

"Hezekiah."

The Marquess of Basin went to bed that night in a daze of happiness. He was fond of animals in general, but the one that had stuck in his memory all those years was that old Bactrian camel on which he'd ridden in the zoo. And now he actually owned one!

He stroked his beard as he settled himself for sleep. And it's a very hairy beast too, he thought.

*

While Hezekiah had been kneeling below the steps to the front entrance of Shortseat, two of the park rangers had put a rope over his neck, one on either side. They prepared themselves for what they imagined would be quite a tussle when the camel got to his feet. But Hezekiah stood quite quietly, gazing at them with eyes as mild as an old Friesian cow. He did make a lot of rumbling noises, though of course they couldn't understand what he was saying.

"Now look, you chaps," he said. "I've come a heck of a long way today and I could do with a good night's sleep."

Which is just what he got, for the rangers decided not to turn him out into one of the enclosures, but to put him, for the time being, in a nice warm old shed, sometimes used to house sick beasts.

After letting him drink his fill from a water

trough, they made him a good bed of straw, and gave him a helping of hay and some interesting roots he'd never seen before. It didn't take long for Hezekiah to decide that he liked mangel-wurzels, and he polished off the lot. Then, with a long sigh of content, he fell into a deep sleep.

He slept so well and dreamlessly that the next thing he knew it was morning. Someone opened the door of the shed and came in. He looked at the man's hairy face and recognized him as the person who had stood at the top of the stairs, dressed in strange clothes.

Lord Basin had risen early and hurried out, still in his night clothes. He wore pyjamas and a dressing-gown and slippers, all very brightly coloured. On his head was a brilliant red woollen nightcap.

"Hezekiah!" he cried.

This was in fact the only word of human language that the camel knew, so often had he heard it. He recognized it as his name. He got to his feet and moved a pace or two towards the Marquess. They looked into each other's eyes, and

perhaps because each was so hairy, both felt that they were kindred souls and had become – and would always continue to be – best friends.

"I expect you'd like to stretch your legs," said Lord Basin. "It's a bit cramped for you in this old shed. Though you can always come back in here to sleep if you like."

In reply he heard the camel make a number of grunty, growly noises. "Any chance I could stretch my legs?" Hezekiah was saying. "This old shed's not all that big. Though I wouldn't mind coming back in here at night."

The Marquess of Basin put out a hand to his Bactrian camel. Something told him that the animal would not bite his hand, and indeed Hezekiah did not. He merely touched it gently with his thick rubbery lips in a kind of kiss.

CHAPTER SEVEN

After Lord Basin had left the shed to begin the important business of dressing up for the day, the rangers came in to fetch the camel. They led him along one of the park's roads to a very large enclosure, a hundred times bigger than his old zoo paddock.

They opened a gate and let him loose inside, but stayed to watch and make sure there would be no trouble with the other animals in there. They didn't expect any bother, but as well as biting, zebras can kick, and so can ostriches, and so can giraffes.

The rangers watched as the other animals moved towards the camel, curious about this hairy beast that carried two humps on its back.

They formed a circle around the newcomer. Hezekiah stood patiently among them, and the rangers, satisfied, moved off.

There were zebras at the zoo – the camel had seen them from his paddock but he had never before set eyes on a giraffe or an ostrich.

"A very good morning to you all," he said (for politeness costs nothing), "and I hope you'll forgive me for trespassing. It's a pleasure to meet you all and before you ask, I'm a Bactrian camel."

At this, one of the little herd of zebras hee-hawed loudly and one of the three ostriches gave out a deep booming noise. Neither of the two giraffes made a sound.

Then the zebra who had neighed said, "Hope you're a vegetarian, mate."

"Certainly I am. Camels don't eat meat."

"Good," said the zebra. "If there's one thing we can't stand, it's a carnivore."

"And we've got plenty of them in Short seat," said another, " as I expect you know."

"Flipping lions!" said a third.

"I thought I heard one just as I arrived yesterday," said Hezekiah.

"There are dozens of the horrible things," said the first zebra.

"Safely fenced in, I trust?"

"Oh yes," said an ostrich. "We can't see them but we can hear them."

"And smell 'em," said the first zebra.

One of the two giraffes curved its very long neck down as though to smell the camel, but it said nothing.

It seemed to Hezekiah to be waiting for him to

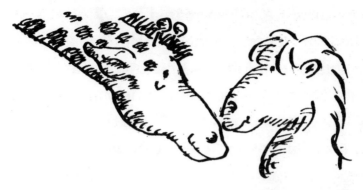

speak, so he asked it, "Do you like living here?"

There was no reply.

"You won't get a word out of him, mate," the zebras said.

"Why not?"

"They can't talk, giraffes can't."

"A female can make a sort of noise to call her calf," an ostrich said, "but they can't speak like we can. Anyway, the answer to your question is – yes, we all like living here. We've got plenty of freedom and friends and food."

"And no foes," chorused the zebras.

In the distance, a lion roared.

"Like him," boomed the ostrich.

The sound of the lion seemed to excite all the animals. The zebras heehawed rudely in reply and set off at a gallop, the ostriches sped away at great speed on their powerful legs that ended in huge two-toed feet, and the two giraffes cantered off gracefully together, in perfect step, like dancers.

Left to himself, Hezekiah walked over to a water-trough that stood by the fence and drank a couple of dozen litres of water. Then he heard the noise of motors and looked up to see a Land Rover coming up the road towards him. It was followed by a van marked in large letters BBC FILM UNIT (which meant nothing to Hezekiah), and after that came a pick-up truck loaded with hay (which meant a lot).

When they drew up by him, there stepped from the Land Rover a bearded figure dressed in riding breeches above bright yellow stockings and suede boots and wearing a cowboy hat.

"Good morning, my friend!" said the camel loudly.

"Feed him!" cried the Marquess to the rangers in the pick-up truck. To the film crew who emerged from the van he said, "Here he is, chaps! Isn't he magnificent? Did you ever see anything so hairy?"

The director, the cameraman and the sound recordist all looked at the camel.

Then they looked at the Marquess.

Then they looked at one another.

Then they replied, "No. Never."

CHAPTER EIGHT

As darkness fell, the rangers came to take the camel back to his shed.

"Hezekiah!" they called, and at the sound of his name, he came immediately to them like a well-trained dog, while the zebras, the ostriches and the giraffes watched.

"Blimey! He's obedient!" said the zebras.

"Knows his name," said the ostriches.

The giraffes of course said nothing.

Hezekiah talked to the rangers as they went down the road. "Pretty tiring day I've had," he said. "Those people kept making me stand here and go there while they pointed things at me and at my friend in his funny clothes. I'll be glad to get to bed."

But before he did, his friend came into the shed to wish him goodnight. Lord Basin was carrying some bananas and he was about to peel one when the camel took it gently out of his hand and swallowed it, skin and all. Five more bananas went the same way, and then Hezekiah sank to his horny kneepads.

"Thanks, my friend," he said, "and now if you'll excuse me, I'll get some sleep. I've had a busy day."

In answer to all his rumbles, Lord Basin said, "Get some sleep, old fellow, you've had a busy day."

A pretty successful day too, said the Marquess

to himself as he went back into the great house of Shortseat. Hezekiah got on well with the other beasts, and I should think the BBC people are pleased with their footage.

As he lay in bed that night, clad in purple silk pyjamas, his red nightcap on his head, he suddenly thought that he should have had a go at riding the camel. That would have looked good on film! he said to himself. But would Hezekiah let me sit on him? he thought. I'm a lot bigger now than when I last had a ride on a camel. Ah well, there's only one way to find out.

Thus it was that next morning when the rangers came to the shed, they did not lead Hezekiah out along the road to his enclosure. Instead they took him into a stable-yard, at one side of which was a stone mounting-block. Standing on this while a horse was led up and stood beside it, it was easy for a rider to step off the block and straddle his steed.

Today the steed was not going to be a horse but (hopefully) a camel. As Hezekiah was led up to the mounting-block, he saw that, standing on it, was his friend, wearing riding breeches and those yellow stockings and various other bright pieces of clothing.

"Now, Hezekiah old chap," his friend said, "I wonder if you will do me a favour?"

He put out a hand to the camel, who gave it that rubbery kiss.

"I shall be so much obliged," said Lord Basin (for politeness costs nothing), "if you'll let me sit on you."

"Tell you what, my friend," said Hezekiah in reply. "Why don't you sit on me and I'll give you a ride?"

What with the kiss and the amiable noises that his camel was making, the Marquess felt confident enough to throw a yellow-stockinged leg over the beast's back.

Hezekiah stood as still as a rock.

Then Lord Basin hoisted himself up off the

mounting-block and sat himself on the broad hairy back, in between the two hairy humps.

Hezekiah did not move.

Lord Basin looked down at his rangers and grinned all over his hairy face.

"How about that, eh?" he said to them.

"Splendid, my Lord," they said. "Shall we lead him on?"

"No, don't bother with the ropes. Just walk on either side of me and then you can open the gate

when we arrive." To Hezekiah he said, "Walk on!"

Being far the tallest, it was the giraffes who first saw the strange procession coming up the road. They could not tell the others, of course, but they cantered over to the fence in such an excited way that the zebras came galloping and the ostriches strode after them.

"Well I never!" said a zebra.

"Did you ever!" said an ostrich.

"Open the gate!" said the Marquess to his rangers.

"Good morning, everyone," said Hezekiah. "I'm giving my friend a ride. He seems to be enjoying it," and he ambled out into the pasture.

The Marquess of Basin sat swaying happily on the camel's back. "Out of the way, you lot!" he shouted to the zebras and ostriches and giraffes, and to Hezekiah, "Trot on!" He took off his cowboy hat and with it gently biffed the camel's flanks. "Giddy-up!" he shouted and Hezekiah broke into a clumsy trot and then the trot became a kind of canter and the canter a sort of gallop.

"Yippee!" yelled Lord Basin as he disappeared into the distance on the back of his big brown bouncing Bactrian camel.

"Well I never!" said one ranger.

"Did you ever!" said the other.

CHAPTER NINE

Later, when Lord Basin had had a shower and changed his clothes, he sat down to his favourite breakfast, a boiled egg. That may not sound much, but it was an *ostrich* egg.

The hen ostriches made no nests but just dropped their eggs on the grass, dozens of them, and the rangers had orders to take one to the Marquess's chef every now and again. The chef would boil the egg for a long time and then, using a small saucepan as an eggcup, set it before Lord Basin, who would eat it with great enjoyment and a tablespoon.

His breakfast finished, the Marquess went to his office. "John," he said to his manager, "I've been thinking."

"Oh yes, sir?"

"About my camel Hezekiah. I've just had a ride on him."

"Really, sir?"

"Yes," said the Marquess. He rubbed his sore bottom absently. Next time, he thought, let's just walk. "I've suddenly realized," he said, "that though he's settled in well at Shortseat and he's healthy and seems quite happy, there is one thing that's missing in his life, and that's a mate. A female Bactrian camel is going to be very hard to find but I want to try, John. I want you to contact every zoo in this country, every zoo in Europe, every zoo in the world indeed, and find out if any of them have a suitable mate for my Hezekiah, and if so, how much they want for her."

"Very well, sir," replied the manager.

Visitors to Shortseat that day found the
Marquess of Basin a trifle abstracted. To be sure,
he moved among them as usual, courteously
answering any questions that they put to him (for
politeness costs nothing), dressed in claret-

coloured corduroy trousers, a mauve shirt with a
saffron cravat, and a sequinned suede jacket. But
they did notice that at intervals he rubbed his
bottom and the more observant among them felt
that the nobleman had something on his mind. He
did. As soon as he could, he returned to his office.

"Any luck, John?" he asked his manager.

"Afraid not, sir."

"No one's got a Bactrian camel?"

"Haven't found one yet."

"Keep trying. Though if we do find a female and if they're willing to sell, they'll ask a huge amount of money. Maybe I can barter for her, but I haven't any more white tigers to spare." Then Lord Basin had a brainwave.

There was a lake at Shortseat, and on the lake was an island, and on the island lived a little family of gorillas, a silverback male, his mate, and their son.

79

"Tell you what, John," said the Marquess. "We need to find a home for our young gorilla."

The phone rang.

"For you, sir," said the manager.

"Hullo?" said the Marquess.

"We are told that you are looking for a female Bactrian camel, and we have one here," said the speaker (and he mentioned the name of a famous American zoo). "It occurred to us that you might be interested in an idea that we've had."

"I might," said the Marquess.

"No doubt you have

the occasional spare creature at Shortseat, and perhaps there's one that might interest us."

"An exchange, d'you mean?"

"Yes, sir."

"All right," said Lord Basin. "How would you like a few lions?"

"No, thanks."

"Oh. Can you hold on a minute?"

"Sure."

The Marquess winked at his manager and held up one hand, fingers crossed.

"I've just had a brainwave," he said to the caller. "How would you like a gorilla?"

"A gorilla!"

"Yes, a young male."

"In exchange for our young female Bactrian camel?"

"Yes. Straight swap. What do you say?" and the answer was:

"Done!"

Chapter Ten

For people to cross the Atlantic by air from America to England (or vice versa) takes very little time. But to transport by sea a gorilla going westward or a Bactrian camel going eastward is not something that can be done in a hurry. So it was springtime before Lord Basin had news of the arrival date of of Hezekiah's proposed mate.

She must have a suitable name, thought the Marquess. I'll consult the vicar.

"Do you happen to know, Vicar," he said to him the following Sunday, "the name of the wife of Hezekiah?"

"D'you mean Hezekiah the King of Judah?" the vicar asked. "Lived about seven hundred BC?"

"That's the one, I expect," said the Marquess.

"As a matter of fact, I do, Lord Basin."

"What was it?"

"Hephzibah."

"Splendid, splendid! I like it!" cried the Marquess. "Could you spell it for me?"

"I'll write it down," said the vicar.

"I've got a camel called Hezekiah, you see, and though he doesn't know it, he's got a mate arriving next week."

"How nice," said the vicar. "Bless them."

"Thanks so much, Vicar," said Lord Basin. "Bye."

*

The spring that year was everything it should
be. The young green grass grew apace, the trees
burst into leaf, the birds were singing their heads
off, the skies were blue, the sun shone.

In the West Country, visitors poured into
Shortseat, to see the famous lions, to see all the
many other animals, and even to catch sight
occasionally of the Marquess of
Basin riding on his camel.
Hezekiah always
kept to a steady
walk now, and
his rider sat
upon a large
comfortable
cushion
wedged
between the

camel's two humps and doffed his cowboy hat to passing visitors.

Now that the weather was warmer, Hezekiah no longer slept in his old shed but stayed out with his companions. There was a lot of hee-hawing as the zebra stallions courted their mares, and a lot of booming as the male ostrich pranced about and flapped his wings before his two hens. The giraffes of course were silent, but they stayed very close to one another, sometimes entwining their long necks in token of their love.

Elsewhere, all the animals of
Shortseat were enjoying the
springtime, from the two
gorillas, alone now on the
lake island, to the herds of
antelopes and the pride of
lions.

Only Hezekiah had no
companion of his own
kind.

One morning when
he was giving his
friend a ride, he spoke
to him about it. "I
wish I had a mate,"
he groaned. "Everyone
else has, but I'm on my tod."
"What's up, Hezekiah?" said the
Marquess. "You sound a bit down

in the mouth. But you just wait, old chap, just wait till this afternoon. You're going to get the shock of your life."

That afternoon (you won't be surprised to hear) Hezekiah got the shock of his life. He was resting comfortably on his horny kneepads beside the water trough, from which he'd just drunk a great deal, when he saw a cattle lorry coming up the road, followed by a Land Rover.

From the lorry a ranger got out and opened the gate and then the driver backed the vehicle into the gateway.

From the Land Rover emerged the brightly dressed figure of the Marquess of Basin, and between them, he and the ranger undid the clips that held up the tailboard, and let it down.

Hezekiah got to his feet, curious to know what newcomer was being put into the enclosure.

"What have you got in there?" he said to his friend the Marquess.

"Guess what we've got in here, Hezekiah old chap!" said Lord Basin. "Come on, Hephzibah, out you come!" Before Hezekiah's astonished eyes, down the tailboard there walked with stately steps a beautiful brown hairy young female Bactrian camel.

"Hullo," she said to him. "I'm Hephzibah. Who are you?"

"I'm Hezekiah," said Hezekiah, and they moved towards each

other till their rubbery lips met in a kind of kiss.

"Love at first sight!" said the Marquess of Basin to the ranger. "I do like happy endings!"

Don't you?

THE END